Iris and the
Aloha Wedding Adventure

For my beautiful Hana

Glossary and pronunciation guide
included on page 81.

Iris and the Aloha Wedding Adventure

By
Lynelle Woolley

Illustrations by
Karen Wolcott

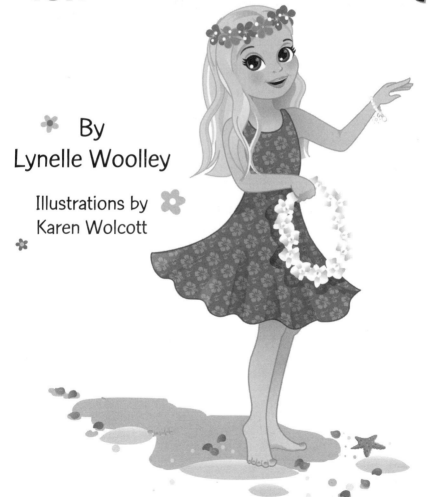

Library of Congress Control Number: 2013910675

ISBN: 978-0-9833116-5-2

Manufactured by Color House Graphics, Inc., Grand Rapids, MI, USA
September 2013
Job #40807
10 9 8 7 6 5 4 3 2 1

www.FlowerGirlWorld.com

Chapter One

"Look at this one!" Iris squealed.

Iris Campbell and her mom were sitting at their kitchen table, looking at a scrapbook Iris had made. The sparkly, purple book was filled with pictures, drawings, and funny messages all celebrating Iris's first experience as a flower girl. Iris had shown this book to her mother probably five hundred times.

"Remember this one?" Iris pointed to another picture.

"Of course I remember. I took that photo, silly girl." Iris's mom smiled.

Iris grinned too. The picture was one of her favorites. It was of her and the two other flower girls, Rosie and Starr. They were eating wedding cake, and each girl had a smear of frosting on her nose.

"You three had so much fun together," said Iris's mom.

Iris, Rosie, and Starr had become very close friends at the wedding. Unfortunately, they all lived in different cities. The girls had formed a club called Flower Girl World and promised to stay in touch. Iris had made everyone Flower Girl World stationery so they could write each other letters. And two different times, Iris's dad had set them up on a three-way video chat.

"I loved being a flower girl," Iris said, pausing on the picture.

"I have some exciting news for you," her mother said suddenly. She went over to the refrigerator and pulled out a plastic bag filled with something pink.

"What's that?" asked Iris.

Iris's mom opened the bag, and the kitchen was filled with a smell as sweet as wedding cake. Inside was a delicate necklace of strung flowers.

"It's called a lei. I made it out of plumeria blossoms," Mrs. Campbell said.

Iris's mom knew all about flowers. She owned a floral and craft store in Philadelphia, where she made beautiful flower arrangements for her customers.

Iris's heart skipped a beat as her mother draped the lei around Iris's neck.

"People get leis when they go to Hawaii," Iris burst out. "Are we…?"

Mrs. Campbell grinned. "Yes, but that's only part of the surprise."

Iris jumped up and screamed.

"What's going on in here?" asked Iris's dad, rushing into the kitchen. "Did we win the lottery?"

"We're going to Hawaii!" Iris bounded over to hug her father and nearly knocked him to the floor.

"Hold on, honey," Mr. Campbell said, laughing. "That's not the whole story."

Mrs. Campbell chimed back in. "Remember when we went to San Francisco last year to see your cousin Jay and his new girlfriend, Malia Lee?"

Iris nodded.

"They're getting married," her mother went on. "The wedding will take place at the Lee family home on the Hawaiian island of Maui."

Iris screamed again. "So we're going to a wedding! Does that mean...?"

"Jay and Malia asked me to make the lei for you as a special gift. They want to know if you will be their flower girl."

Iris threw her arms in the air. "Are you kidding? Yes!"

"Malia has two younger sisters. Leilani, the older one, will be her bridesmaid. The younger one will be a flower girl with you. Her name is Hana."

Iris's smile grew even bigger.

"One last part," her mother added. "This is a very big deal."

"Lori, I don't think Iris can handle any more excitement," Mr. Campbell said, winking at Iris.

"Dad! Stop it! Mom! Go on!"

"We've been asked to arrive a few days early to help set up and decorate. We will be picking flowers, creating the wedding arch, making the leis and centerpieces..."

"OMG!" Iris was now jumping up and down and clapping.

"Honey, the wedding is six months away. Maybe you should save some excitement for later," said her mother.

But Iris couldn't wait. She immediately ran out of the kitchen and up the stairs.

"Where are you going?" her dad called after her.

Iris shouted back, "I have to tell Rosie and Starr that I'm in another wedding. And that Flower Girl World is about to get a new member!"

Chapter Two

"Come in the water, Dad! It's not cold at all!"

It was six months later, and Iris was up to her ankles in the Pacific Ocean, waiting for her father to finish putting on his sunscreen. As she waded through the water, the wet sand felt soft and squishy between her toes. Iris smiled. *This place is nothing like Philadelphia*, she thought.

Iris and her family had arrived in Maui early that morning. The plane ride was so long that Iris was able to read a book, watch two movies, play three games of Crazy Eights with her dad, and knit a scarf before they landed. Even though she was sleepy, Iris was ready to start her vacation right away. As soon as her suitcase was delivered to their hotel room, Iris put on her swimsuit and dragged her father to the beach.

"Dad! Hurry up!" Iris shouted. She looked over at her father and noticed he was talking to a young couple. Iris's heart jumped.

"Jay! Malia!" Iris ran toward her cousin and his bride-to-be.

"Hello, my pretty flower girl!" Jay said, picking her up and twirling her around.

"So when can we start making decorations for your wedding?" Iris blurted out.

Malia laughed, but Jay pretended to groan. "Oh, Iris," said the groom. "Do we have to talk wedding stuff already?"

"Believe me, it's all she wants to talk about!" teased her father.

"Dad!" Iris blushed. "Talking wedding stuff is fun!"

"I agree!" said Malia. "I'm so happy you're here. I can't wait for you to meet my sisters."

"Me too! Where are they?" asked Iris.

"Out there." Malia pointed to the ocean.

Iris spotted two young girls on surfboards riding a cresting wave. The taller girl glided

calmly through the water. But the smaller one shot through the waves, weaving in and out at a lightning pace.

"Whoa!" Iris said. "They're really good."

Malia caught her sisters' attention and motioned for them to come in. When they made their way back to the beach, Malia introduced Iris to them.

"Aloha!" said the younger girl, Hana. Her white smile glistened against her tan skin.

"Welcome to Maui," added Leilani.

"Thanks! It's nice to meet you," Iris replied.

"Malia told me you've been a flower girl before," Hana said. "This is my first time. I'm so excited."

"I'm excited too!" said Iris. "I want to give you something."

Iris bent down to rummage through her beach bag. She pulled out a sparkly, pearl-beaded bracelet. "This is for you. I made it."

Iris placed the bracelet on Hana's wrist. Hanging from it were two charms: one was shaped like a flower, and the other was oval and had the letters FGW painted on it.

"I love it! Thank you!" said Hana. "What does FGW mean?"

"Flower Girl World. It's a club all about flower girls. Now that you're in a wedding, you're an official member."

Iris told Hana about Rosie and Starr and how much fun they had had being flower girls together.

"Flower Girl World connects every girl who loves being a flower girl! Even girls who have never been in a wedding!"

"That's so cool!" said Hana.

"I'm sorry to interrupt," said Malia.

"Hana, we have to clean up before the luau."

"Luau?" asked Iris.

"We're all coming back here to your hotel for a big party tonight," said Jay. "There will be Hawaiian food and a hula dancing show."

"You'll meet my parents, and that's when our families will talk about the plans for setting up the wedding," said Malia.

"Great," said Iris.

"And don't forget," Hana chimed in. "She'll meet Tutu too."

"Who's Tutu?" Iris asked.

Hana and her sisters exchanged looks and giggled.

"You'll find out tonight," said Hana as she turned to go.

Chapter Three

Rumble, rumble, boom!

Five pretty hula dancers wearing grass skirts shook their hips wildly.

Rumble, rumble, boom!

Men draped in Hawaiian print fabric stomped across the stage. Each carried a large stick, its ends lit on fire.

Iris and Hana looked at each other with wide eyes. They were sitting in the front row at the luau show, excited for what would happen next.

Rumble, rumble, boom!

The men threw their fire sticks in the air like batons.

Iris gasped!

Boom! Boom! Boom!

On stage, a large ring was set aflame. One by one, each man dove through the ring. They tumbled into a forward roll

before standing up again. But that wasn't all. A second ring was set on fire. The last man in line would be diving through both hoops at the same time!

Iris could barely watch. She covered her eyes but left a little space between her fingers for peeking.

A powerful drumroll pounded, and the brave dancer took a running start…one ring…two rings…He did it!

Iris and Hana stood up and cheered. "That was awesome!" Iris shouted.

Hana nodded. "Leilani and I are doing a hula dance at the wedding. It's our gift for Malia and Jay. Do you want to be in it too?"

Iris didn't have to think very long. "No way!"

Hana looked surprised "Are you sure? It'll be fun!"

"I'm not a good dancer," Iris explained.

"One time, I had to dance in a school show. I twirled the wrong way and landed on a lady's lap in the front row!"

The girls hooted with laughter until a thundering voice made them jump.

"WHAT'S SO FUNNY?"

Iris turned to see a plump woman with tightly curled short hair. She was wearing a sack dress with big orange flowers. Her eyes narrowed as she glared at Iris and Hana. Iris gulped.

"Aloha!" Hana cheered. She ran over to the woman and threw her arms around her. "You missed dinner and the show. It was the best luau ever!"

Iris was confused. *Why is Hana talking to this scary lady?* she thought.

"Iris, this is Tutu, my grandma," Hana said.

Tutu's angry scowl quickly turned into a warm, beaming smile. "Nice to meet you, honey! Hope I didn't scare you!"

"Oh!" Iris sighed as the color returned to her face. "It's nice to meet you, Tutu. I like your name. Were you a ballerina?"

"Ha-ha!" Tutu burst out laughing as if the image of Tutu in a tutu was very funny. "Tutu is an island nickname for Grandmother," she said. "Kind of like Nana."

"Our family is a mix of many cultures – Chinese, Japanese, Hawaiian," added Hana. "My name means flower in Japanese."

"A flower name is perfect for Flower Girl World!" said Iris.

Hana beamed proudly.

"Okay, that's enough chitchatting," Tutu roared, startling Iris again. Tutu put her arm around the girls' shoulders and led them over to their parents. "It's time for wedding work!"

Chapter Four

Iris, Hana, and their families gathered around the large table where they had met earlier for the luau meal. There were many adults present, but Tutu was clearly in charge.

"The wedding is in three days," she said. "That means we only have two days to finish everything."

Worried looks spread across the table.

"If we work together, everything will get done. Here's the plan…"

Tutu began by barking orders to Iris's and Hana's dads. "Men, you need to rent the guest chairs and set them up on the beach."

Then she glanced at Iris's and Hana's moms. "You're in charge of decorating the tables, chairs, and grounds."

Next, she focused on Malia and Jay.

"You two meet with the judge, DJ, and

jeweler to finalize everything."

Then she took a deep breath. "I will cook the food. And if you all know what's good for you, you'll stay far away from my kitchen!"

Tutu had a special way of being funny even when she seemed angry. Everyone chuckled – except Iris. She was disappointed that she, Hana, and Leilani weren't given jobs. Iris turned to Hana, but her friend wasn't at the table. Instead, Hana was turning cartwheels on the grass.

Mrs. Lee noticed too. "Hana!" she said. "Get back over here."

Hana stopped turning. "Why? Tutu didn't give me a job."

Tutu chimed back in. "You, Leilani, and Iris are in charge of making the leis. Tomorrow, I will take you to pick flowers in the local gardens."

Iris's heart skipped a beat. She couldn't wait for tomorrow morning. She glanced at Hana, who rolled her eyes.

"Excuse me," interrupted Iris's mom. "I'm concerned. We have a lot to do in two days."

"Don't worry. We'll get it all done," Tutu assured everyone. "And if we run into problems, the *Menehune* will help us."

Hana quickly perked up at the sound of this funny word.

"Many who who?" echoed Iris.

"It's pronounced *Meh-neh-hoo-neh*," corrected Tutu. "They're happy little island creatures, kind of like leprechauns or elves.

They help people finish big jobs. In fact, they built the entire Hawaiian Islands."

"Mother!" Hana's mom interrupted. "That's a legend."

Hana jumped in. "*Menehune* live in big trees. They only come out at night when everyone is asleep. No one has ever seen one."

"Do you really think they'll help us?" asked Iris.

"Of course!" exclaimed Tutu. "This wedding is as important as all the Hawaiian Islands combined!"

"Mother!" Hana's mom shook her head with a slight smile.

Iris turned to Hana, who was now grinning widely.

"This is going to be fun!" Hana said.

Yes, it is! Iris thought.

Chapter Five

Iris closed her eyes and inhaled deeply.

The scents of all the tropical flowers mixed together to create a perfume as sugary as cotton candy. Iris licked her lips, wishing she could eat petals for lunch!

Iris, Hana, and Leilani were in a local garden, collecting flowers for the wedding leis. The sun was warm, but a slight breeze and the shade of the trees kept the girls cool. Iris was plucking an orange and pink plumeria blossom, when some leaves dropped on her head. She looked up, expecting to see an exotic bird or a

Menehune, but instead…

"Hana!" Iris laughed. "What are you doing up there?"

Hana was stretched across several limbs, grabbing flowers. As she moved, more leaves fell to the ground. Iris noticed that the branches bent under Hana's weight.

"The best flowers are on the top," claimed Hana as she climbed higher.

Leilani ran over. "Hana, get down! You know Mom doesn't let us climb trees!"

"I'm not that high!" Hana crawled further.

"Do you want to get hurt before the wedding?" Leilani asked.

"Fine!" Hana climbed out of the tree. "I was only trying to have some fun while I worked."

"Yes, but that's when you get into trouble," said Leilani.

Hana crossed her arms and scowled.

"Remember your famous 'dishwashing dance,' when you broke Mom's favorite platter? Or when you decided to play with the hose instead of cleaning off the patio? You flooded the backyard!"

Hana shook her head and walked away from Leilani.

Iris approached her. "Are you okay?" she whispered to her friend.

Hana shrugged off the question while she pulled some blossoms off a low-hanging branch. For the rest of the morning, Hana stayed on the ground, but she also kept to herself.

Later, everyone met at the Lee home to work on wedding tasks. Iris, Hana, and Leilani sat on the patio, stringing sweet-smelling leis. From her seat, Iris could see her mom and Mrs. Lee on the lawn, making an elaborate wedding arch out of hibiscus flowers. Out on the beach, her dad and Mr. Lee were setting up white chairs along the sand.

It's so beautiful here, Iris thought.

All of a sudden, Hana cried out in frustration. "Agh! These flowers don't work right."

Iris noticed that Hana was covered in torn petals.

"I think it's you who doesn't work right," teased Leilani.

"Ha-ha," Hana replied, not amused. She tried again to string a few more blossoms. When the petals crumbled in her hand, she threw everything to the ground.

"These leis are a waste of time," she muttered. "Leilani, let's practice our hula."

"*You* can practice our hula. I have to finish making leis," said her sister.

"Fine!" Hana replied, stomping off. "Watch me!"

Out on the lawn, Hana began to shake her hips. She started slowly but quickly picked up the pace. Iris couldn't believe how fast Hana could move her hips without moving her top half at all. Then Hana began to turn. At first she twirled in place, but then she began moving across the lawn. She kept shaking and turning and moving faster and faster…

"HANA!" everyone suddenly shouted as she danced near a table set up for the wedding reception.

But the warning came too late. Hana's flip-flop caught hold of the tablecloth, and she pitched forward, taking the cloth and the vase of flowers with her.

Hana's mother ran over. The young girl was covered in soggy flowers and a wet pink tablecloth.

"Are you okay?" Mrs. Lee asked while helping her stand.

Hana nodded.

Then her mother's tone changed. "No more playing around! Do you want to get hurt before the wedding?"

Iris realized it was the second time someone had asked Hana that question that day.

Hana looked down. "I'm sorry."

"We don't have time for games," her mom scolded. "Go to your room so the rest of us can get our work done!"

Chapter Six

Iris finished another lei before going upstairs to Hana's bedroom to check on her friend. She found Hana lying on her bed, her head hidden underneath a big, sparkly pillow. Iris immediately recognized the picture on the pillow. It was Gaby Snow, the world's biggest pop star. Iris was a huge fan.

She sat on the bed. "Hana, I have good news."

Hana didn't stir.

"Our moms said I could sleep over tonight."

"Really?" Hana popped her head out from the pillow.

"On one condition…" Iris grabbed the pillow from Hana. "I get to sleep with the Gaby Snow pillow!"

Laughing, the girls started a playful pillow fight. Iris was glad to see Hana smiling again. But as soon as their game wound down, Hana's happiness faded.

"I didn't mean to cause trouble," said Hana as she wiped away a tear.

Iris nodded.

"I want to help with the wedding, but when will we have time to play?"

"After we finish all the work," said Iris.

"Wait a minute," Hana said. She had a glint in her eye. "We need the *Menehune* to help us. Once everything is done, our parents will be happy and we can have fun!"

"How are we going to do that? You said the *Menehune* only come out at night when no one is around."

"We'll capture one!" exclaimed Hana.

"Huh?" Iris was confused.

"It'll be easy!" claimed Hana. "We can set a trap this afternoon."

This plan was moving too quickly for Iris. "Why don't we try working faster on our own?" she suggested. "I can help you make your leis."

"No, my idea will work. What can we use to lure the *Menehune* to our trap? I know – a cookie! Everyone loves cookies!"

Iris couldn't deny that last part.

Hana exclaimed, "Let's get started!"

Iris didn't know what to do. She liked making leis, but she didn't want to disappoint her new friend.

Iris took a deep breath. "Okay, let's do it."

Chapter Seven

The girls crept into the kitchen. Tutu was too busy stuffing a chicken to notice them. Hana quietly opened the door to the large pantry, and they sneaked inside. It was dark and smelled like cereal, but Hana knew her way around. She easily found all the materials they needed to build their trap: string, a square cardboard box, and an open container of vanilla wafers.

"Vanilla wafers are perfect!" Hana whispered. Iris nodded silently.

To avoid Leilani on the back patio, the girls went outside through the front door and ran past their parents to the far end of the property. This area was full of lush trees and plants. Iris spotted a large tree with roots hanging down from its branches like long pieces of spaghetti.

"What's that?" she asked.

"It's a banyan tree," Hana told her. "I bet a bunch of *Menehune* live in it!"

The girls decided that the base of this tree would be the best place to set their trap.

Iris found a sturdy stick. Hana tied string to one end of it and used the other end to prop up the cardboard box. Then they placed two vanilla wafers under the trap.

"Now what do we do?" asked Iris.

"We come back at midnight."

"What?!!" Iris's stomach suddenly hurt.

"We have to catch the *Menehune* tonight, so everything will be done tomorrow. It's not dangerous," she added. "Leilani and I camp out here all the time."

Iris arched her brow.

"Don't you want to be one of the first people in the world to see a *Menehune*?" asked Hana.

Iris thought for a second. Catching a *Menehune* would surely make her famous. She'd probably be in the newspaper and on TV. And maybe she'd even get to meet the mayor of Maui!

"But what if we get caught sneaking out?" Iris asked. The thought of an angry Tutu gave her the shivers.

"We won't! We'll sneak out quietly and be back in a flash."

Iris bit her lip. "Alright," she said slowly.

Hana took a cookie out of the box and popped it in her mouth. "Want one?" she asked as she chewed.

Iris shook her head. There wasn't enough room in her belly with all the butterflies.

Chapter Eight

It was midnight. Hana and Iris popped their heads out of Hana's bedroom door. All was silent…except for loud snoring coming from Tutu's room.

The girls tiptoed along the hall, down the back stairwell, and quietly opened the back patio door.

The night was warm but windy. Air whistled through the palm trees as it blew leaves from side to side. Passing dark clouds dimmed the light of the thin crescent moon.

Iris trembled. "Maybe we should go back inside," she told Hana. "It's spooky out here."

But Hana was already heading toward the banyan tree. "Don't worry. There's nothing to be afraid of." She shined the flashlight and moved quickly ahead.

Iris didn't want to be left alone. "Wait for me!"

By the time she caught up, Hana was by the trap. The look on her face told Iris that something was going on.

"What's wrong?" Iris asked. She was out of breath.

"I think we caught one." Hana shined the light directly on the trap.

The box had fallen forward and it was moving slightly from side to side. The girls were inspecting it, when a sudden squeal came from inside. Both girls gasped.

"Now what do we do?" asked Iris.

"I don't know!" Hana exclaimed. "I guess we should take a peek."

She slowly reached down to lift up the box and –

Boom!

At that very moment, there was a loud thunderclap and a flash of lightning. Both girls screamed, and Hana dropped the flashlight on top of the trap. The light went out, leaving the girls in total darkness.

Boom! Crackle! Boom!

Another burst of thunder and lightning tore through the sky. And that's when heavy drops of rain began to fall.

"Let's get out of here!" cried Hana. She picked up the flashlight, but the light wouldn't turn on.

"What about the trap?" asked Iris.

"We'll come back tomorrow in the daylight," replied Hana, who was already running toward the house. Iris did her best to keep up.

The girls were drenched by the time they reached the kitchen. They used dish towels to dry themselves off.

"That was scary!" Iris said.

"Can you believe we caught a *Menehune*?" Hana asked.

Iris shook her head. At that moment, all she cared about was being safe inside the house.

"I'm so excited!" Hana declared. "Tomorrow, our *Menehune* will finish all the work, and we'll get to have some fun!"

Chapter Nine

The girls woke to warm sunshine streaming through Hana's bedroom window – and loud noises outside. From their beds they could hear people shouting and stomping heavily around the house.

"What's going on?" asked Iris.

"Maybe it's a *Menehune*!" said Hana. They leaped out of bed and ran to the window. Iris expected to catch a glimpse of the magical creature. Instead she saw something that shocked her even more.

The backyard was a disaster. Everything that had been set up for the wedding had been destroyed in the storm. Fallen palm leaves covered the ground. The white folding chairs were caked with sandy mud. The beautiful wedding arch that the girls' mothers had made was ripped apart.

"Oh, no!" shouted Iris and Hana together.

The girls ran downstairs to the kitchen. They found Tutu throwing containers of food into garbage cans.

"Tutu!" Hana exclaimed. "What's happening?"

"Everything is ruined. We lost power in the middle of the night, and all the food spoiled. Your leis will have to be thrown out too."

She held up one of the leis. The beautiful pink and orange plumerias were now brown and wilting. Iris did her best to hold back tears.

"It doesn't make any sense," Tutu said, shaking her head. "The forecast predicted a beautiful night. But that storm was awful!"

Hana and Iris exchanged glances.

"Now what?" Hana asked nervously "The wedding is tomorrow."

"We have to start over," answered Tutu.

Hana and Iris's mouths dropped open. They both knew what they had to do: get help from the *Menehune*!

Arriving at the banyan tree, the girls hoped to find the *Menehune* but instead discovered more of the same mess. Small trees had toppled over, leaving broken branches everywhere. The cardboard box trap had been blown to one side of the banyan tree, while the stick and string were on the other. There was no sign of cookies or a magical creature anywhere.

For a few moments, neither girl spoke. Finally, Iris broke the silence. "What do we do?"

Hana shook her head. "Like Tutu said, we start over."

Tutu dropped Hana, Iris, and Leilani off at the flower field to collect more plumeria for the leis. The garden looked completely different from the day before. The trees were practically bare. Instead, petals and leaves were scattered all over the ground.

"This place looks really bad too." Hana said. Her voice quivered. "I think this is our fault."

"Me too," agreed Iris.

Leilani overheard them. "What are you talking about?"

"We caused the storm," said Hana. "Last night we caught a *Menehune*."

"What?" asked Leilani.

Hana told her about their plan to get the work done more quickly. She described how

they had built the trap and sneaked out of the house to check it at midnight.

"I think we made him angry!" said Iris. "Now he's punishing us and making bad things happen."

"Will Malia and Jay's wedding be ruined?" asked Hana.

Leilani chuckled and shook her head. "*Menehune* aren't real, silly. Like Mom said, they are part of a legend. You probably caught a gecko in your trap!"

"Do you really think so?" asked Iris hopefully.

"I'm sure," replied Leilani. "Now let's get back to work. There have to be some plumeria here that we can still use for the leis."

The girls split up in search of fresh flowers, but it wasn't easy. "I can't find any!" Iris declared.

"I found some," Hana yelled from somewhere out of sight.

"Where are you?" shouted Leilani

"Up here!" Hana had climbed high up a tree and was stretching to reach some plumeria far out on a branch.

Iris and Leilani ran over to the tree.

Leilani yelled, "Get down! It's too dangerous!"

"I'm fine. Look how pretty these are."

Hana stretched her arm out toward the brightly colored petals.

Snap!

The branch cracked, and Hana started to tumble down. Thinking fast, Leilani moved underneath the tree to catch her sister.

Thud! Hana fell, knocking Leilani over.

"Oh, no!" Iris cried. She ran over to Hana and Leilani. They were both lying on the ground. "Are you okay?" Iris asked.

Hana slowly rolled over. She was able to move her arms and legs. "I'm not hurt, thanks to Leilani. She broke my fall."

Iris looked at Leilani, who had tears streaming down her face.

"I think my ankle is broken!" Leilani cried out.

Chapter Ten

In the waiting room at the hospital, Hana and Iris huddled together on a bench next to Tutu. Leilani and her parents were meeting with a doctor in another room.

Tears filled Hana's eyes. "This is all my fault," she whimpered. "Leilani's leg, the storm, the spoiled food, the ruined decorations. I feel terrible."

"It'll be okay," comforted Iris.

"What?" Tutu narrowed her eyes as she overheard them. "How could all this bad luck be your fault, Hana?"

Iris exchanged a glance with Hana. "Well…" Hana began, "we…"

Tutu listened as the girls told her the whole story about catching a *Menehune*.

"I see," Tutu said. For a long time she didn't say another word. Then she cleared her throat.

"I'm glad you girls told me what you did. Hana, you know better. You should never leave the house late at night without getting permission from an adult. I hope you have learned your lesson. The *Menehune* are not to be messed with."

"But Tutu, is there anything we can do to make things better for the wedding?" Hana asked with a sniffle.

"You already broke the rules, and we can't turn back time. But…" Tutu gave the girls a stern look. "From now on, cooperate and be extra-good helpers. We have a wedding to save!"

Hana's grandmother hugged both girls. "One more thing. Put some more vanilla wafers out for the *Menehune*. You have to keep them happy."

"But Leilani said the *Menehune* aren't real," said Hana.

"What could it hurt?" asked Tutu.

Iris and Hana exchanged looks and shrugged. They were finally smiling again too.

Just then, Leilani entered the waiting room with her parents. She was using crutches to walk.

"We have some good news and some bad news," Hana's dad said.

"Leilani's ankle isn't broken," said her mom.

"Whew!" Hana sighed in relief.

"But it is badly sprained," she went on. "It's wrapped in a tight bandage, and she'll have to use crutches."

Iris swallowed hard. "What about the

wedding tomorrow? How will she walk down the aisle?"

"We'll decorate the crutches with some flowers," said Hana's dad. "We'll make the best of it."

Hana turned to her sister. "I'm so sorry. I didn't mean to hurt you."

"I know. You were trying to help the wedding," Leilani said. "I forgive you."

Hana smiled. Iris began to feel better too.

"Speaking of the wedding, we have a lot of work to do," Tutu said.

"Wait a minute," Leilani interrupted. "What about the hula? I won't be able to dance. Oh, no, Hana. It was our special gift to Malia and Jay!"

"What are we going to do?" Hana wailed.

"No worries!" Tutu declared. "Iris can take Leilani's place."

All eyes turned to Iris. She felt her face heat up.

"No way!" Iris blurted out. "I can't do the hula. I'm a terrible dancer! There's no time for me to learn. The wedding is tomorrow!"

"Please, Iris!" begged Hana. "I can teach you. It's for Malia and Jay."

Iris was having trouble swallowing. How could she possibly learn a dance in one day?

"Nope! No way! Can't do it!" she repeated.

Everyone was still looking at her. Iris could see sadness in all their faces.

"You can do it, Iris," said Tutu calmly. Then she whispered into Iris's ear, "Don't forget, the *Menehune* will help you too."

Iris gulped. She didn't know what to do. *I wish Rosie and Starr were here to help me decide*, she thought. But she already knew what they'd say.

"Alright," she said softly.

"Hooray!" the family cheered.

Hana hugged Iris. "Thank you! Don't worry, you'll be a great hula dancer!"

Iris wanted to believe Hana, but she couldn't help worrying. Everything in this wedding had gone wrong so far.

Chapter Eleven

There was no time to waste! When the family returned to the house, everyone went right to work. A neighbor had heard about Leilani's accident and brought over baskets of fresh flowers. Now the girls were remaking all the leis.

When she finished her first lei, Hana proudly held it up for all to see. "Look! I'm ready to make another one."

"Wow!" Leilani said. "It's perfect!"

Iris was amazed at how quickly Hana had strung the flowers. And she hadn't broken any petals!

When all the leis were finished, Hana and Iris asked their fathers if they could help them with their jobs. The girls raced each other to see who could set up more chairs on the beach. Then they offered to help their moms with the decorations. Hana folded napkins while Iris arranged flowers in vases.

With no more tasks to complete, the girls headed to the banyan tree to make things right with the *Menehune*. They decided to

leave a whole box of cookies as an apology
gift. Hana wrote a note. It said:

> Dear *Menehune*,
>
> We are SO sorry! Will you
>
> forgive us?
>
> Mahalo, Hana & Iris
>
> P.S. We hope you like the cookies!

"What does Mahalo mean?" Iris asked Hana.

"It's Hawaiian for 'thank you.' If we're
polite, maybe they'll be nice again."

"I hope so!" agreed Iris.

After dinner the girls met on the back
patio. It was the moment that Iris had been
dreading all day: the hula lesson.

"You can do it, Iris!" cheered Leilani
from a chair.

Iris scrunched up her nose as if she
smelled something rotten.

"Don't worry. I'll help you," said Hana. "Every hula dance tells a story. The movements are the words of the story."

"Our hula is about love," added Leilani. "Hana will dance, and I'll explain what each step means."

Hana opened her arms to the sky.

"*It comes from the heavens.*"

Hana leaned over and swept her arms to the ground.

"*It's as deep as the ocean.*"

Hana crossed her hands on her chest.

"*Love is in your heart.*"

Hana opened her arms wide in front of her.

"*Spread it around the world.*"

"That's it," said Hana. "We repeat it until the music ends."

Iris clapped her hands. "It's so pretty! And it looks easy!"

"Now we'll teach you how to turn and move your hips at the same time," said Leilani.

Iris's smile dropped to the ground.

"Try it with me," said Hana.

The girls practiced together. Iris learned the arm movements quickly, but the other parts weren't so simple. Sometimes she

would move her hips to the right, but she'd forget to turn to the left. At one point, she became so tangled up, she tripped over her feet and fell.

"Are you hurt?" asked Leilani.

"No," said Iris. "Just embarrassed."

Hana reached down to help Iris stand. As she pulled her up, both girls yawned.

"It's getting late. We should go to bed," Leilani suggested. "Tomorrow is a big day."

"All you need is sleep, Iris," Hana said "Then your dancing will be perfect."

Iris wanted to practice some more, but she could barely keep her eyes open.

"Okay," she said uneasily.

I need more than sleep, she thought. *I need a big miracle!*

Chapter Twelve

BAM! BAM! BAM!

Loud smacking noises jolted Iris and Hana from their sleep.

"Oh, no!" exclaimed Iris.

"Not again!" cried Hana.

The girls threw off their sheets and ran downstairs to the kitchen. There, they found Tutu knocking a jar against the counter, trying to loosen a tight lid.

"Good morning!" Tutu sang. "No problems today! Everything is set up and ready for the wedding." Then she winked. "I guess those apology cookies worked."

"Yay!" The girls launched into a happy dance. For a second, they did not realize there was another person in the room.

"Good morning," someone said.

Hana and Iris froze. Standing before them was a beautiful bride. Malia wore a wreath of white orchids in her hair. The fabric of her elegant white gown was printed with faint Hawaiian flowers.

"Wow…" said Iris. "What a beautiful dress!"

"You look so pretty!" Hana said.

"Mahalo!" replied Malia.

"I can't wait to see you two wearing your flower girl dresses!"

With all the activity over the past few days, Iris had almost forgotten the best part of her Hawaiian trip – being a flower girl!

"What are we waiting for?" Iris asked Hana. "Let's get dressed!" She darted up the stairs past her friend.

"Wait for me!" yelled Hana.

A few hours later, Iris and Hana stood on the beach in pink, breezy sundresses, waiting to walk down the aisle. Pink plumeria petals were spread all over the sand before them, leading to the beautiful hibiscus wedding arch that the girls' mothers had repaired.

Iris and Hana were bubbling with excitement. Instead of dropping more petals on the aisle, the flower girls had been given a different task: Iris was carrying the lei that Jay would give to Malia, and Hana carried the one Malia would give to Jay.

"It's a Hawaiian custom," Hana had explained earlier. "It's like exchanging rings."

"Wow," Iris said. "We have a really important job."

Jay and the ceremony judge stood at the other end of the aisle under the arch. Leilani was there too, leaning on crutches decorated with lush tropical flowers. As a light ocean wind blew, the first sounds of the wedding music began.

"That's our cue," said Hana.

Iris's heart leaped as she took her first step with Hana. *I love being a flower girl,* she thought.

Reaching the end of the aisle, the girls turned to watch the bride walk behind them.

Malia looked like a Hawaiian princess as she glided past the guests.

The girls held on to the leis until it was time to give them to the bride and groom. Jay winked at Iris when she passed him the white orchid lei. She could tell he was filled with joy as he placed it around his bride's neck. And Malia looked the same when she gave the green leaf lei to her groom.

As the ceremony continued, Iris eagerly awaited the most special wedding custom of all – the kiss! When the couple's lips met, everyone cheered.

What an awesome wedding! Iris thought as she walked back down the aisle with Hana. But when everyone headed to the reception area for the party, her happy feelings faded fast.

Uh-oh! she thought. *It's time for the hula!*

Chapter 13

"Aloha! May I have your attention, please?" Leilani requested.

Balancing on her crutches, Leilani spoke to all the guests in the reception area. A hush spread across the crowd.

"Congratulations, Malia and Jay! As our gift to you, your flower girls, Hana and Iris, will perform a special hula dance."

Iris gulped when she heard her name. She wanted to duck under a table and hide!

Hana grabbed Iris's hand and led her out to the dancing area. "You'll be great, Iris," she whispered. "Don't forget to have fun."

At the first beat of the Hawaiian love song, Iris managed to take a step to the right. Another beat, and she shyly moved her hips to the left. Then, when the tempo of the music picked up, Iris finally had no choice. She had to dance!

> *It comes from the heavens.*
>
> *It's as deep as the ocean.*
>
> *Love is in your heart.*
>
> *Spread it around the world.*

Phew! Iris finally let out her breath. She had performed the first round of the hula perfectly. But there was no time to congratulate herself. She had to do it again!

The music for the next verse started to play. Through all her jumpy jitters, Iris suddenly realized something – she was having fun. And the more she danced, the more fun she had. With their hips shaking and arms flowing, Iris and Hana repeated the dance again and again. Soon, all the guests were on their feet, dancing the hula with them.

When the music stopped, there was an explosion of clapping. Iris beamed.

I did it! she thought. *And without any help from the* Menehune!

Hana turned to Iris. "You were great! I'm so lucky you're my friend, Iris. Thank you so much!"

"I'm so lucky you're my friend, Hana. Mahalo so much!"

The girls giggled and hugged. They knew that they'd be friends forever through the special bond of Flower Girl World. Suddenly, their amusement was interrupted by a familiar booming voice.

"WHAT'S SO FUNNY?"

The sound made Iris jump, even though she knew it was Tutu.

"Why are you two standing around? It's dessert time!" Tutu barked. "After your wonderful performance, you deserve a piece of my famous pineapple upside-down cake!"

"I get the biggest piece!" cried Hana.

"Not if I get there first!" Iris joked.

The flower girls dashed for the dessert table.

"Mmm…" Iris said as she took her first bite.

"Smile!" The girls looked up to find Mrs. Campbell pointing a camera at them. "Let's take a picture for your Flower Girl World scrapbook. You can send a copy to Rosie and Starr too."

"Wait!" Iris said. Then she put a little of the cake's sugar topping on the tips of their noses. "Now we're ready."

"Say Aloha," said Iris's mom.

"ALOHA!" cheered the two flower girls.

Iris flashed her biggest smile. From the luau to the hula and everything in between, she loved her incredible Hawaiian wedding adventure.

GLOSSARY AND PRONUNCIATION GUIDE

Hawaiian Terms

ALOHA (*ah-loh-hah*) – Hello or farewell

LEI (*lay or lay-ee*) – A wreath of flowers or leaves that can be worn around the neck or head

LUAU (*loo-ow*) – A Polynesian feast that can include traditional island foods and entertainment

MAHALO (*mah-hah-low*) – Thank you

MENEHUNE (*meh-neh-hoo-neh*) – Mythical island creatures

Flowers

HIBISCUS – (hi–bis-kus)

ORCHID – (or-kid)

PLUMERIA – (ploo-mare-ee-a)

Names

HANA – (hah-nah)

LEILANI – (lay-lawn-ee)

MALIA – (mah-lee-uh)

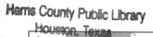

Visit us at
www.FlowerGirlWorld.com

Awesome Activities!

Great Games!

Creative Crafts!

Hip Hairstyles!

Terrific Tips!

Sensational Stories!

Tell your friends about Flower Girl World!

Together, you can start
an FGW club, trade the books,
stage a pretend wedding,
and create lots of fun!

FLOWER GIRL WORLD™